THE MICAH ROAD MYSTERIES
THE SECRET ORDER

by Sara Lynne Hilton

Copyright © 2013 by Sara Lynne Hilton

Special thanks to editors: Amy White, Jan Boone, Gert Wolfert

Published by GEMS Girls' Clubs, a division of Dynamic Youth Ministries
Grand Rapids, MI

Visit us at: www.gemsgc.org

GEMS Girls' Clubs is an international, non-profit organization. For the past fifty-four years we have been ministering to women and girls around the world through club programs and other faith-based types of outreach that demonstrate what it means to act justly, love mercy, and walk humbly with God.

Requests for information should be addressed to: Micah Road Mysteries, GEMS Girls' Clubs, PO Box 7259, Grand Rapids, MI 49510.

Educators and librarians, for a variety of helpful tools visit us at: www.gemsgc.org/mrm

This book is a work of fiction. Any similarities to real persons, living or dead, is coincidental and not intended by the author.

All rights reserved. No part of this book may be reproduced, stored in a retrieval system, or transmitted in any form or by any means—electronic, mechanical, photocopy, recording, or any other except for brief quotations embodied in critical articles or reviews or by written permission of the publisher.

ISBN 978-0-615-74033-1

Cover and interior illustrations by Elisa Chavarri
Layout and cover design by Tina DeKam and Kelly Werner

Printed in the United States of America

For Hailey Grace and Tyler Matthew

Table of Contents

chapter 1	The Escape	7
chapter 2	Ten Paces from Each Door	8
chapter 3	Ghost Village	15
chapter 4	The Spiders	22
chapter 5	The Code	25
chapter 6	They Didn't Have a Chance	30
chapter 7	Three Swords	39
chapter 8	Hunters Lurk Nearby	44
chapter 9	The Fortress	50
chapter 10	The Revenge of Jeremiah Plum	53
chapter 11	Hunted	58
chapter 12	A Once Haunted Land	62
chapter 13	Walker Door Day	69
chapter 14	It Isn't Funny	77
chapter 15	The Fires	83
chapter 16	Almost Midnight	87
chapter 17	Expelled	92
chapter 18	The Face of Hate	96
chapter 19	Light	98
chapter 20	Quiet	100
chapter 21	Freedom	103
chapter 22	The Box	107

Prologue

WHERE WE LEFT OFF...

The following Saturday, Tasha and I planned a relaxing weekend. I slept in, and then I walked to her house for lunch. After lunch we made our famous triple chocolate cookies. And, because you can never have too much chocolate, I made some of Zocha's hot chocolate to wash the cookies down. We carried a tray of cookies and hot chocolate to our office where we planned on spending the afternoon doing absolutely nothing.

But life doesn't always turn out like you plan.

Someone had stuffed an envelope under the door. I set down the tray and picked it up. The front of the envelope had cut and pasted letters from a magazine to spell out:

Open Now.

Tasha and I exchanged worried glances, and I carefully opened the envelope and pulled out a letter. As I opened it, paper, cut into triangles, stars, and squares, fell to my feet like confetti. Tasha bent to pick them up as I looked at the letter. It was written in the same cut and pasted letters as the envelope.

I read it out loud to Tasha.

I cannot Tell You WHO I am, but If you don't help me, ShE could DiE. Don't try to Find mE. Wait For my nEXT LEtTer.

It was signed,

-The AgEnt.

One

....

THE ESCAPE

Tasha grabbed my arm. I didn't need to be told what to do. We went back to the stairs, not to hide, but to escape. We ran up the twisting stairs. The dark upward spirals made me sick to my stomach, but we couldn't stop. We had already seen too much, heard too much, risked too much.

I could hear footsteps behind us. We climbed faster, but the spiral stairs felt endless, as if we were trapped in a nightmare of infinite steps. It felt like we'd never escape—like we'd never find the top of the windowless Fortress.

Two

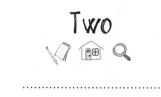

TEN PACES FROM EACH DOOR

Three days earlier...

Power is deceiving. It's not always the biggest or loudest thing in the room. I didn't know that when this all started. I didn't know that sometimes the quietest thing has the most strength, or that you have to search a bit before you recognize that it's been there all along—like the quiet hum of power lines.

For two weeks a person who called himself The Agent had been sliding clues under our office door. Tasha and I take our job as detectives very seriously, and The Agent's first letter had been so urgent that we devoted everything we had to helping him. So for the last two weeks we had followed his clues. For the last two weeks we studied and researched and carefully followed every lead. For the last two weeks we turned away other cases (two lost cat cases and one lost parakeet) to focus on The Agent. But here we were—two weeks in and sitting on nothing more than a random pile of facts and a whole lot of frustration. We kept detailed notes about the clues in our case file:

{CASE FILE}

aRt liVEs HeRe
lefT haLL   *EVIDENCE Clue #2*
BAttleScraWL

Detective Brainstorm:
Where does <u>art</u> live?
* School Art Room
* Art Books
* The University
* Art Museum

Which one of these places has a <u>left hall</u>?
* The University
* (The Art Museum) !

Visit to Tenebray Art Museum

* We turned to the left as soon as we entered. There was a hallway leading to an exhibit room. One painting showed a Civil War battle. Battle Scrawl!

★ Hypothesis:

* The clues have something to do with <u>the Civil War</u>! But what does that have to do with us? With The Agent? ???

Two weeks of work and all we had was The Civil War, Frosted Loop Cereal, and nails. Not much of a case. So, I'll be honest, when we arrived at our office to find a new clue under our door, I was pretty irritated. Tasha picked up the envelope with the cutout letters OPEN NOW on the front.

"How much longer are we just going to keep following these clues?" I asked. I thought about the two missing cats and missing parakeet cases we had turned down. We could have spent the last two weeks actually helping people instead of searching through cereal boxes. "For all we know someone is just messing with us. Someone was probably at the grocery store getting a laugh watching us search in the Frosted Loop Cereal section. I'm starting to think this isn't even a real case."

"I don't know," said Tasha, "maybe if we follow enough clues they will start to make sense." Tasha never does anything without thinking it through first, and she hates giving up on something. I guess that's what makes her such a great friend. She'd never give up on me, even though sometimes I probably deserve it. But sometimes strengths and weaknesses get mixed up. Refusing to give up is a great thing, unless someone is refusing to give up on something that was never real in the first place—like a fake case.

"Tash," I said. "I know how you feel about sticking with things, we just need to make sure we are sticking with the right thing."

Tasha was quiet for a moment. "Okay," she finally said, although she still sounded reluctant. "How about this: one more clue, and if it doesn't lead anywhere, we'll stop."

"Fair enough," I said.

"But you have to promise to really do this last clue. You need to really help me and not just get through it so you can quit."

"Fine," I answered. "I promise. Now open it."

Tasha ripped open the envelope and took out the paper inside. The clue, like the others before it, had been cut and pasted from magazine letters.

Northern tenebray
Jeremiah Plum
ten paces from each door.

"Who's Jeremiah Plum?" I asked.

"He was the founder of Tenebray," said Tasha.

"How do you know that?" I asked.

"How do you not know that?" Tasha responded.

I shrugged and opened my laptop. I did a search on Jeremiah Plum's name, and clicked on the first link. It was a book excerpt of some sort. Tasha read it out loud:

In 1850, Jeremiah Plum led thirteen families to Tenebray's northern region. Under Plum's guidance, a small settlement was formed. However, the land in the northern region consisted of large rock beds and did not sustain farming. Upon Jeremiah Plum's death in 1862, the settlement was abruptly moved to the southern portion of Tenebray where land was more suitable for farming. This second settlement is the loction of Tenebray's current town center.

The article went on for several pages and detailed what life was like in the first settlement.

"Nothing about Frosted Loop Cereal?" I joked.

"I think some of the old cabins are still there," Tasha said, ignoring my cereal comment. "Can I see your computer?"

I slid it her way and she did a search for a map of the first Tenebray settlement.

"Isn't it strange that no one ever goes to the first settlement?" I asked while Tasha searched. "You'd think we'd go there on field trips or something."

"Hmmm," said Tasha. "I don't know." She found a map that showed the original placement of each cabin and each owner's name. She printed it, and put it into her backpack.

"Ready?" she asked.

I didn't answer. I knew she wanted to walk to the settlement, but, no, I wasn't ready. I had gone through libraries and museums and grocery stores for The Agent, and I was done—I had no interest in wandering around some old buildings. But I said, "Ready," anyway. I wasn't doing this for The Agent anymore. I was doing it for Tasha—one more clue for my friend who never gives up.

I stood and put on my backpack. We locked our office door behind us and began walking toward northern Tenebray and toward a clue and a discovery that would change our town forever.

Three

GHOST VILLAGE

Jeremiah Plum's settlement had decayed into a ghost village. Some of the roofs had caved in and those with remaining shingles were in the process of peeling away like a snake shedding its skin. A few roofs sagged and rose like waves. The glass had been broken out of most of the windows, many chimneys had crumbled, and the wood had turned into a smooth gray color—like the color of sickness.

We stood on a large rock about twenty feet in front of the decaying settlement while Tasha studied the map. It was easy for me to imagine life within the empty homes. The decaying village still had the feel of a small town. The cabins were so close together that there couldn't have been much privacy. The article had stated that about sixty-five children lived in the small settlement. I imagined how much noise sixty-five children must have made. I sat down on the rock while Tasha figured out which house belonged to Jeremiah. I dragged my foot across the gravelly dirt. Why would they settle so far from farmable land?

"I don't understand why people listened to Jeremiah," I said. "Why wouldn't people just ignore him and go where farming was easy?"

"I don't know," answered Tasha. She looked up from the map. "Maybe people were afraid of him. It would explain why nobody moved until after he died." Tasha looked at her map again. "Jeremiah's house was exactly in the center of the settlement," she said. "There should be six cabins on either side of his house."

We counted the cabins, or what remained of them anyway, and then walked toward the house that stood directly in the middle. It was certainly the largest of the homes and the only one made of brick. It had a large front door with ornately carved doorposts like on a church. But the grand entrance was comically out of place on the small, dilapidated home. There was a star on the door handle.

"Stars are one of the things that fell out of The Agent's first letter," said Tasha.

I took out my phone and snapped a picture of the handle for our case file. You never know what might be important. Then we entered Jeremiah Plum's cabin. We were immediately blinded by the quick transition of a sunny fall day to the cool darkness. The smell inside was repulsive. It was a little like wet dog mixed with rotten vegetables.

When our eyes adjusted we didn't see anything impressive. Although Jeremiah Plum's house was the biggest of the settlement homes, it was still very small. The main floor consisted of one large room. The far wall had old cupboards and shelves, and we guessed it had served as the kitchen. Two loft spaces had been built above the main living area. These upper rooms were only accessible by ladders. I guessed that one loft was used for the children and one for the parents. According to the records, Jeremiah Plum and his wife, Constance, had eight children.

We searched the old home, and I tried to imagine what life must have been like for Jeremiah and his family.

"How could ten people live in this house?" I asked.

"How'd they stay warm in the winter?" Tasha wondered. Tenebray's winters were long and harsh. One fireplace didn't seem like enough.

"It doesn't make sense," Tasha said. "Ten paces from each door, but...."

"There is only one door," I finished, pausing for only a moment before continuing. "But maybe there's a secret door."

Tasha looked skeptical but was willing to search. We circled the cabin, pressing on the walls, but found nothing.

"It was a good thought," Tasha said.

"Maybe I was right all along," I said. "Maybe

someone is playing with us." This time the thought scared me. Tasha didn't respond, so I said it again. "Maybe we are being tricked."

She said nothing.

"Tasha?" I asked. "Did you hear me? I said…."

"What's that?" Tasha pointed toward the wall with the cabinets.

"I think that's the kitchen, remember?" I responded.

"Yeah, I know," she said, "but look at the wall." She walked over and pointed. "What are these?"

I looked closely and could just make out the remnants of what looked like old hinges. "Hinges?" I guessed.

"That's what I thought," answered Tasha. "And if there are hinges, that means there used to be…."

"A door!" I answered.

"A door," she repeated.

"But that doesn't make any sense. Why would there be a door on the wall? What's the point of a door that doesn't lead to anything?"

"I don't know," answered Tasha. "But let's just say it was a door. You stay here and I'll go back to the actual door. Let's both count ten paces."

Tasha ran across the room to the front door and then turned to face me. "Ready?" she asked.

I nodded, and we counted as we stepped toward each other, "One, two, three…." I felt the excitement that always comes when we find a clue. It was like a good hand in a game of cards. You know you have something amazing, and you can hardly wait to lay it down. What would we find at the count of ten? Would something open? What would be revealed?

"…nine, ten." We stopped, nose to nose in the middle of the room. We looked up and down and right and left, but there was nothing. Nothing happened; we didn't see anything—just two girls looking ridiculous standing nose to nose in an old cabin.

"Well," I said, "that was amazing. How about the floor? Maybe there's a loose floorboard with something hidden underneath." I got down on my knees. The boards had buckled and were bent with age, but still firmly secured to the floor. No matter how hard I pried, the boards were stuck. I stood, frustrated.

"Look!" said Tasha. She pointed to where I had been kneeling. My knees had cleared the dust from the floor and revealed a small carving of a sword. "Maybe this is the loose board," she said.

We knelt together and pulled, but, like the others, it wouldn't budge. We sat on the floor, defeated. I actually felt kind of bad. I guess deep down I hadn't wanted to quit either. I guess I really had wanted to solve this case, too.

"Any ideas?" I asked Tasha.

"None."

"You know," I said, "if this agent person is really so desperate, he could try being a little more specific. Does he actually want help?" My phone dinged with a text. It was my mom asking me to stop and get milk on the way home.

"How is she?" Tasha asked while I typed back a message.

I shrugged. "Some days are worse than others." I put my phone back into my pocket. "So now where should we look?" I wanted to change the subject. I didn't want to cry, not here. "What does the sword mean?"

"Chloe?" Tasha asked. "You okay? Do you want to talk about it?"

I shook my head.

She stood and looked at me for a moment. I could tell she wanted to help, but she knew me well enough to give me some space. "Maybe the sword is some sort of seal or art or…." She paused and then asked, "What if it's an arrow?"

"I don't understand," I said.

"The sword," she answered. "What if it's like an arrow and points in the direction of something?" She stood and looked in the direction that the tip of the sword was pointing. If it was an arrow, then it was pointing to the crumbling stone fireplace. When we approached the fireplace we quickly found another engraving of a sword. The sword was located at knee height and pointed up. Our eyes moved toward the ceiling, but there were no more carvings.

At first glance it looked like a small stone had fallen out of the chimney. The small, deep hole was just about at my eye level. Then I realized there was another small hole about twelve inches across from the first one. I hooked a finger into each small hole and pulled it open like a drawer. A square piece pulled out of the chimney and revealed a long, rectangular opening. Tasha pointed her flashlight inside, but the space was a tangled net of spider webs.

Neither of us wanted to reach into that dark, web-infested hole, so we played rock, paper, scissor—best of three. I lost. I took a deep breath and reached into the webs. They stuck in clumps between my fingers. I tried not to think of the rats or mice or bats that might have made this space their home, and I tried to convince myself that the spider webs wrapping around my fingers were old and spiderless, but no matter how hard I tried to believe myself, I was sure I felt hundreds of spiders crawling over my arm. *It's just your imagination*, I told myself over and over. And then, when I had reached in as far as my shoulder, I felt it.

Four

THE SPIDERS

"I feel something," I said to Tasha.

"Can you pull it out?" she asked.

My fingers were just able to grasp the edges of an object. "I think it's a book," I said.

I gently pulled the object forward. The sensation of spiders was getting worse, and I wanted it to be over—I wanted to see my arm and know that the spiders were all in my imagination. But they weren't. They were real. When I pulled my arm out of the hole, there were hundreds of real baby spiders crawling up my arm, working their way past my shoulder to my neck and around my back. I screamed, and the book I was holding dropped to the floor with a dusty thud.

I tried wiping the spiders away with my hand, but they were fast, and in seconds they were everywhere. It almost seemed like they were multiplying. Tasha grabbed my spiderless arm and pulled me outside. "Try rubbing your arm on the gravel!" she yelled.

I fell to my knees and scraped my arm and shoulder and back on the loose dirt and stones. Tasha stood over me and tried to brush them away "Don't let them get in my hair!" I screamed. From far away we must have looked insane—two girls fighting an imaginary foe. But the foe was real. The spiders were everywhere.

I don't know how long we frantically removed spiders, but even after Tasha circled me a dozen times and assured me they were gone, I could still feel them crawling all over me. It was as if my body just couldn't let the feeling go.

"They're gone," Tasha finally said when I asked her to check for the thirteenth time. You just have to believe me."

"I can still feel them," I said.

"Well, your body is lying to you, because they aren't there. You're okay," she said. "They're gone." And then she gave me a long hug. "Would I hug you if you were covered in spiders?" she asked.

"Probably not," I said.

"Do you believe me now that they are gone?"

I nodded. She let go, and I tried to memorize the feeling of her hug instead of the creeping feeling of the spiders.

"Wait here," Tasha said. She went back into Jeremiah's house and came back seconds later holding the book. A few small spiders still hung to the pages so she quickly dropped it on the gravel. The book was yellowed with age, and at first glance the cover seemed to be blank. But when Tasha brushed off the dust and the last few spiders, something was revealed.

"What language is that?" I asked.

"I don't know," Tasha replied. She gently opened the book. It was handwritten in the same strange symbols as the cover.

"How are we supposed to read this?" I asked.

Tasha just smiled. "Filip."

Five

THE CODE

"All we need to do is create the cipher for the code." Filip was in our office, paging through the book. Filip was our friend, but at one time he had been our client. He came to us when he was accused of committing a crime in Tenebray Forest. We were able to help him and in the process became very close. We thought of Filip as a brother.

One of the things I loved about Filip was the way his brain worked. He could look at a problem, easily see the broken parts, and then invent a way to fix it. So when we showed him the book, he quickly decided what was needed: a cipher.

"What's a cipher?" I asked.

"Well, for starters, I'm pretty sure this isn't an actual language. I think it is some sort of secret code."

I got a chill. *Secret code*? Whatever this was, someone had gone to a lot of trouble to keep it hidden. What secrets were tucked away in those mysterious symbols?

Filip continued. "A cipher is the key to a secret code."

"Where do we buy a cipher?" I asked.

Tasha giggled, "I think Filip means we need to make the cipher."

"Exactly," said Filip. "Every secret code is different, so each code needs its own cipher."

"So how are you going to create a cipher to this code?" I asked.

"Trial and error," he answered. "If this is a simple code, then each symbol would represent a letter in the alphabet. So I'd start by guessing. For instance, I'm going to start by assuming that the symbols are chunked together to make words, and that spaces between the chunks of symbols indicate a new word. The title of the book has three symbols in the first chunk. What is a common three-letter word in titles?"

"The," said Tasha.

"Right," he said. "So I start by assigning the letters T, H, and E to those symbols. Every time those symbols appear I know what letter they represent. Then I just play around until I can figure out what letters go with what symbols. Eventually, I'll be able to translate the whole book."

"You said that's how it works for a simple code," I said. "What if the code isn't simple?"

"Then it gets a lot harder and will take a lot longer. Sometimes ciphers can be many codes deep. If it's okay with you, I can take the book home tonight and work on it. I can let you know in the morning what I find."

"Someone worked really hard to keep whatever is in that book a secret," I said. If there was one thing I had learned from our last case it was that secrets never want to be exposed.

"It's also obviously a very old secret," said Filip. "Whoever wrote this couldn't possibly be alive anymore."

Maybe it was just the spiders talking, but something about the book felt current and alive. "Why would The Agent lead us to the book if it didn't mean anything?" I asked. "I can't explain why, but I feel like we need to be careful."

"Okay," said Tasha. "I agree."

Filip nodded. "So let's make some rules. We don't walk around with the book in public. We hide it in a bag or something."

"Perfect," said Tasha. "And, for now, we keep the book between us. No talking about it at school or to friends."

"And we work quickly," I added. "We can't forget the first message. Someone might be in serious trouble."

We all agreed. Filip stashed the book in his backpack. "I'll call you," he said and then left for home.

Tasha and I spent a few minutes making notes about

our trip to Jeremiah Plum's house so we wouldn't forget anything important. Good detectives need to be concerned with details, even the ones that don't seem significant. When we finished our case files for the day, I hugged Tasha goodbye and started the walk home.

I walked quickly. All I wanted was to take a hot shower. No matter how hard I worked to convince myself the spiders were gone, I still felt them. Every little itch made me wonder if one was still hiding inside my sleeve or in my pant leg. I couldn't wait to throw my clothes in the washer and take a hot shower to scrub everything away. As I walked I thought about Jeremiah Plum. I wondered if people had stayed in the first settlement out of fear. What had this man done to make everyone so afraid? Why hadn't people just told him no? I wondered if sometimes fear felt like the spiders. After one experience it is hard to convince yourself that you don't have to be afraid anymore. Maybe Jeremiah Plum did one really scary thing to make people follow him. Maybe people kept following him because they just kept being afraid.

When I got home I went straight to the bathroom. The water from the shower felt amazing. I turned it up as hot as I could stand, and I washed my hair three times—just to be safe. But the shower didn't wash everything away. Something was lingering. It was as if I had absorbed something from Jeremiah's house—absorbed some of that fear. And with everything that had been happening with my mom, I knew a lot about fear.

I texted Filip to make sure he made it home okay. He had.

He said he was in his room working on the cipher. But that didn't make me feel better. Somehow I just knew that the book was about to reveal something bad. What I didn't know at the time was just how big that something was or just how close it would come to each one of us.

Six

THEY DIDN'T HAVE A CHANCE

The next day, Tasha and I went back to Jeremiah Plum's house to see if we could find any more clues. The instant we entered I felt the tingle of the spiders. I asked Tasha to check me over. She assured me the spiders were just my imagination.

We walked to the far wall to investigate the door-like hinges.

"Let's assume there used to be a door here," said Tasha. "The hinges are in the right spots to hold a door, and the clue about the paces matched."

"But why a door that opens to a wall?" I asked.

"Maybe to hide something?" Tasha suggested.

"Or someone," I added.

We checked the area for loose wallboards, but the wall was just a wall.

Tasha's phone rang. "It's Filip," she said. She talked for a few minutes, and then gave him directions to Jeremiah Plum's house. "He's meeting us here. He said he found something important."

I nodded and turned my attention back to the mysterious doorway-to-nothing. "I guess you could hide papers behind a door that leads nowhere, but there isn't space for anything big."

"Let's leave it for a few minutes and look around," Tasha suggested. Maybe we'll find something that helps us explain it."

Other than the mysterious doorway, the cabin was pretty boring. Tasha brought a broom. She swept the floors looking for more carvings while I checked the walls. We didn't find anything.

"How about the lofts?" I asked.

"I don't know," said Tasha. "This house is so old."

"It's been around for over 150 years. It's solid," I said. I went over to the ladder that led to the front loft. I put my flashlight in my back pocket. "Spot me," I said as I started to climb.

Tasha held the ladder. "Chloe," she said, "I don't like this."

I ignored her and quickly made it far enough to peek into the loft. "The floor is rotten in some areas," I said. "I'll have to just look around from the ladder."

"Hurry," said Tasha.

I shined my flashlight around the space. It was empty, dusty, and full of cobwebs. "Nothing," I said as I climbed down. "Let's check the other one."

Tasha didn't protest this time. Instead, she said, "My turn."

"You don't have to," I said.

She didn't answer. She just started climbing. I held the bottom of the ladder. "Can you see anything?" I asked when she was high enough to look into the loft.

"No," she answered. "I don't know how eight kids could have slept in here. I'm coming down."

As Tasha stepped back with her right foot, the rung under her left foot cracked. She slipped down two more rungs before falling backward onto me. We landed in a heap on the floor.

"Are you okay?" I asked.

"Yep," said Tasha. She rolled into a sitting position. "You?"

"Yeah," I said. "Maybe you were right about those ladders not being so safe."

She laughed. So did I. I looked to my left and saw a spider tending to its web with its front legs. I jumped up and brushed off a few more imaginary spiders.

Tasha stayed seated and stared at the mysterious doorway. "Where's the door?" she asked.

"Um, right there?" I pointed to the hinges.

"Yeah, I know. But where is the actual door? Why is the door missing?"

"Hey." Filip walked into the cabin. "I cracked part of it," he said. "Some of it was only one cipher deep, some of it goes a lot deeper. I don't have a lot translated yet, but there is something you need to see."

We sat in a circle on the floor. Filip set the book in the middle, and I stared at the strange symbols on the cover of the book I had fought off spiders to obtain. I felt repulsed by its symbols and yellowed pages.

Filip pointed to the title. "*The Secret Order*. That's what this says."

Hearing *The Secret Order* made me wish we had met back at the office and not in Jeremiah Plum's cabin, not in the very place where the secrets had been hidden.

"*The Secret Order* of what?" Tasha asked.

"I think of slave hunters," Filip answered.

"Excuse me?" I asked.

"Stick with me," he said. "I found something that links to your case, but you have to understand the history first. I think this book is a record of how this *Secret Order* captured runaway slaves. I've only had time to translate bits and pieces, but I do know that the entry dates in this book go from 1850 to 1862."

"Jeremiah Plum died in 1862," Tasha said. "Do you know if he wrote it?"

"I don't know yet," said Filip. "But it seems to have entries about slaves this group caught, and there are money amounts by the slave names. I think the money is the reward money."

"Reward for what?" I asked.

"For returning the runaway slaves to their owners," answered Filip.

"But slavery was illegal here in 1850," said Tasha.

"Right," answered Filip. He pulled a pack of papers out of his backpack and shuffled through them. For as brilliant as Filip was, he was the most disorganized person I had ever met. He searched a bit longer and then handed a piece of paper to Tasha. "It didn't make sense to me either, so I did some research last night." He pointed to the paper. The top read, *The Fugitive Slave Act of 1850*.

"By 1850," he continued, "states in the northern United States had made slavery illegal. But states in the southern United States still allowed slavery. This was a problem for the southern states because slaves were escaping to the north. So in 1850 the United States passed this law that said slaves who escaped to the north could be tracked down and returned to their owners."

Filip pointed to highlighted text. "Read this," he said. He handed Tasha a printout. I moved closer to her to read.

The Fugitive Slave Act of 1850

The Fugitive Slave Act of 1850 made it very difficult for a slave to find freedom, even in free states.

1. It was the duty of all federal officers (police) in both free and slave states to capture and return runaway slaves. Officers who captured slaves were entitled to bonuses (extra money) and promotions.

2. Officers who failed this duty were subject to a $1,000 fine.

3. No evidence was needed to capture and return a runaway slave. If an owner claimed a person belonged to him, the slave was to be returned. The slave had no rights under the law and could not protest being taken into slavery.

4. Any person helping a runaway slave could be sentenced to six months in prison and a $1,000 fine.

"They didn't have a chance," said Tasha. "Even if they made it to a free state…."

"They could be hunted down and returned," I finished.

"After the law was passed, slaves had to make it all the way to Canada to escape the slave hunters," said Filip.

"But that was like over 800 miles for some of the slaves," I said.

"On foot," added Tasha. "But back to *The Secret Order*. You think these people were hunting down runaway slaves? What does that have to do with us?"

"Well," said Filip. "First of all, Tenebray is a boarder town. From what I translated, I think a group of Americans and Canadians were working together. It was illegal for slave hunters to work in Canada, but that didn't always stop them. Sometimes they just kidnapped runaway slaves from Canada and brought them back to the United States to get the reward money. Tenebray would have been the perfect place for this. Think about it: the United States side tries to keep slaves from crossing over, and the Canadian side guards their boarder and captures slaves that do make it. Each time someone caught a slave, they all made money."

"So they used human slaves to get rich?"

"I think so," said Filip. "Right now it's just my hypothesis. I need more time to prove it."

The idea of this was so beyond anything I could imagine. How does a person buy and sell and kidnap and enslave another person? Was I sitting in the home of someone who had done such horrible things? We sat quietly for a moment and let the sick possibility of Tenebray's history sink in. I hoped more than anything that Filip was wrong. I loved Tenebray. It was my home.

After a bit, Filip interrupted my thoughts, "There is something else. I think it's important. It's about *The Underground Railroad*."

The Underground Railroad wasn't really a railroad. It was a secret organization of people from both the United States and Canada who helped slaves escape slavery. I thought about the details of *The Fugitive Slave Act* I'd just learned and realized for the first time how dangerous it was to help runaway slaves. Just helping someone escape could mean going to jail. I wished this book of symbols had been part of *The Underground Railroad*—part of a secret history I could be proud of.

"*The Underground Railroad* had code words," continued Filip. "They used them so they could talk about what they were doing without being caught. Like Canada was known as 'Heaven' or 'the promised land.'" Filip shuffled through his mess of papers until he located another sheet. "I found this list of code words and what they mean. Read all the way to the end."

Tasha picked up the paper, and I read over her shoulder.

Code Word: Load of Potatoes

This meant slaves were hidden in a wagon under produce.

Code Word: Passengers/Freight/Cargo

Escaping slaves—males were referred to as "hardware" and females as "dry goods."

Code Word: Stations

Temporary safe-houses where slaves hid along the escape route. They could be churches, barns, or houses.

Code Word: Station Master

The keeper of the safe-house or station.

We read all the way to the bottom of the list before understanding why Filip had showed us, before understanding that somehow the dark history of Tenebray had come out of the past and into our lives. I read it in disbelief. It couldn't be a coincidence. There among the definitions was the code word for the person who operated *The Underground Railroad* and made routes for the escaping slaves. It was a code word we had become familiar with over the past weeks. I read it three times before I looked up.

"Tasha?" I asked. "What does this mean?"

"I don't know," she said.

I looked down to read it one more time. There it was, in black and white:

Code Word: The Agent

Seven

THREE SWORDS

"So let me get this straight," I said. "The Agent in *The Underground Railroad* was the one who planned how slaves would escape?"

"Yes," said Filip.

"And someone who calls himself The Agent has been leaving us clues that led us to this book about slave hunters."

"Yes."

"The first clue from The Agent said, 'she could die,'" Tasha pointed out. "This isn't just about history. What if something in this history is supposed to save someone now? Filip, did you translate anything else?"

Filip nodded. He slid a piece of paper across the desk. "I translated some entries last night, I don't know if it has anything to do with the case, but from what I can tell, these two names keep popping up more than any other names."

Tasha picked up the piece of paper and read it aloud.

October 26, 1853
Captured: Slave woman named Eliza. Age: 26
Reward upon return: $100
Captured: Female slave child, Basil-daughter of Eliza
Age: 5
Reward upon return: $100

Eliza is the property of Jerrett Worthington of Georgetown, South Carolina. Eliza is said to have run after sale of Basil to Arthur Ackland of Sumpter, Alabama. Slaves are to be separated and returned to their respective owners.

I stared at the paper. "Was Basil Eliza's daughter?" I asked.

"Yes," said Filip.

"Why were they going to separate them?" I asked.

"Slave children didn't belong to their parents," explained Filip. "They belonged to the slave owner. Owners would often sell kids to other slave owners to make money."

"She was five." I said. I looked up at Tasha. Her face looked as sick as I felt. "What kind of person sells a five-year-old girl and separates her from her mother?"

There was no need to answer. We all felt the coldness of someone who could do such a thing. I thought about the five-year-old girl I babysat and how sometimes she cried when her parents left. It never took long for me to distract her, but she knew her parents were coming back. I couldn't imagine what it must have been like for Basil to be sold, taken away from her mother, knowing she'd never see her again. I don't know if I was more sad or angry, or maybe I was just a muddy mix of both. Eliza and Basil had made it all the way to the border. That meant they had walked hundreds of miles toward Canada, toward freedom. This mother and daughter had walked to stay together. They risked their lives to stay together. Within the horror of the story I could feel the strength of their love—a love that had carried them hundreds of miles to freedom. The grief of being caught right at the last minute, right before freedom, must have been unbearable.

"What happened?" I asked Filip. "Does it say what happened to Eliza and Basil?"

"I don't know," he answered. "I'll keep translating."

I resolved then to crack the case. I would crack it for Eliza and Basil. I wanted to reveal to the world what Jeremiah Plum had done. I couldn't save Eliza and Basil, but I was determined to find them at least an ounce of justice by revealing Jeremiah Plum for what he really was.

"There is one more thing," said Filip. "I don't know what this means, but this sign keeps appearing throughout the pages." He opened the book and showed us several examples of some sort of logo. Three swords formed a triangle. Inside the triangle there was an image of a fist, shackles, and a torch. Whatever the sign meant, it didn't look friendly.

Tasha leaned in and took a closer look. Then she looked up at us and said, "I know that sign."

Eight

HUNTERS LURK NEARBY

We went back to the library—back to the south corner, to the adult nonfiction section, back to the very place The Agent had first led us. Tasha found the book, *Civil War Recreated*, and pulled it off the shelf. "There," she said.

We all leaned down and looked into the space where the book had been. In the very back, etched into the wood, was the symbol of the three swords.

"I didn't really think anything of it when I saw it the first time. I just thought it was some seal from the people who made the shelves. But when Filip showed it to us…."

"That's what The Agent is trying to get us to see,"

I said. "We have to recheck the other locations for the symbol." I had no idea what the symbol meant, or why it was important, but it couldn't be a coincidence.

We took the Civil War book to the front desk, and Tasha handed it to the librarian along with her library card. The librarian took the book, put it underneath the counter, and slid Tasha's card back to her. "This book is not for checkout," she said.

"Why?" I asked. "It was on the shelf with the other books."

"I would be more than happy to show you kids some books in the youth section."

"We want this one," I said.

"I'm afraid that isn't possible," she answered. She reached under the counter, took the book, and walked with it into the back room.

"Should I follow her?" I asked.

"I don't think that's a good idea," said Tasha. "Come on. Let's go."

Once we were outside Tasha said, "Filip, can you go home and keep translating? It suddenly feels like we need to move as quickly as possible."

"Absolutely," Filip answered.

"Chloe is right, now that we know what we are looking for, we need to go back and revisit all the locations. We'll call you."

Filip left for home, and Tasha and I walked to the art

museum—the place of the second clue: *Art Lives Here. Left Hall. Battle Scrawl.* We went back to the large image depicting a U.S. Civil War battle. We checked the walls around the painting, the benches in the room, even the doorframes, but we found nothing. No symbol.

"Could it be somewhere in the painting?" I asked.

"Great idea," said Tasha.

We stood in front of the large image and studied it carefully. Tasha searched for clues on the side of the Northern Union soldiers. I studied on the side of the Southern Confederate soldiers. I tried to look at the picture with new eyes. I looked for the symbol in the grass, in the trees, in the clouds—anywhere it might be hidden. We stood there for so long the images seemed to lose their structure. The painting no longer looked like anything, just colors and patterns and shapes. I would have missed it if it hadn't been so hot in the room. I unbuttoned my jacket, which gave me the idea.

"There!" I shouted to Tasha.

"Miss!" scolded the museum curator who happened to be walking by. "Please be quiet."

I apologized and then whispered, "There. Look at that soldier's buttons."

Tasha leaned in to where I was pointing. The Confederate general was sitting on a horse behind his soldiers. Each of the buttons on his coat was marked with the three-sword symbol. Tasha held up her phone to take a photo, but the curator grabbed her arm.

"No photographs," he said.

Tasha nodded and put her phone into her pocket. "Let's go," she whispered.

The curator watched us leave. He didn't say goodbye.

The rest of the afternoon was similar. At the grocery store we found the symbol behind a shelf sticker. At the hardware store we found it carved into the shelf underneath a selection of nails. At each location someone was there, looking over our shoulders and telling us to leave.

By the end of the afternoon we knew two things: one, The Agent wasn't leading us on a wild goose chase. Two, whatever this secret was, it was heavily guarded.

I called Filip as we walked back to the office. He said he had emailed us the most recent translations regarding Eliza and Basil and to call him if we had questions. I begged him to give me the details over the phone, but he said it would be much better for me to read them myself. I knew that whatever he had translated had already happened. It was the past. It was done. I didn't have any power to change what happened to Eliza and Basil. But their lives were affecting me as if it were happening now.

Tasha offered me a snack from her backpack, but I wasn't hungry. My fear and sadness over Eliza and Basil's separation made me physically sick to my stomach. How could either one of them survive after they were separated? I suddenly felt a deep ache to hear my mom. I called her. She sounded chipper on the phone even though yesterday was a chemo day, and I knew she was feeling horrible.

I knew she was putting on a front for me. I knew she was trying to protect me from the way her sickness had changed all of our lives. She was being strong for me even though she was the one in pain. I wondered if Eliza was strong for Basil like that.

When we reached the office, I went right to the laptop and clicked on the file from Filip and read it aloud.

Runaways Eliza and Basil held in Walker's barn. Approximately 8 AM, riders prepared to deliver woman and child to respective owners. Upon entry of barn, slaves were discovered missing. Dogs released, but no scent was found. Woman and child remain at large.

"They escaped!" I yelled. I gave Tasha a hug. They had done it. The strength of Eliza's love had been enough after all. I started to cry, which is strange because I hadn't cried for a long time. I hadn't cried when my parents told me about the cancer or when my mom lost her hair or even when she went to bed and months later was still there. I think maybe when things are really bad the tears get stuck. I pulled away from Tasha and put my face in my hands, but Tasha pulled me back and hugged me tighter. She didn't say anything. She let me do the one thing I really needed to do. She just let me cry.

Then I heard the swish of paper and saw the familiar envelope with the clipped-lettered writing, OPEN NOW, appear under the door. Tasha ran to the door, but there was no one there. She closed it and bent to pick up the clue. She read it aloud:

**CINDERBLOCK WALLS
PAINTED WHITE
NO DOORS OR WINDOWS in SIGHT**

"The school walls are cinderblock," I said, wiping my tears on my sleeve.

"But there are windows and doors everywhere," Tasha answered. She handed me the clue. I didn't see it at first. It was written so lightly. On the very bottom of the clue, scrawled in tiny, penciled letters was the message:

Beware. Hunters lurk nearby.

Nine

THE FORTRESS

"What exactly are we being warned about?" I asked Tasha. "Approaching slave hunters?"

Tasha took the clue and studied the penciled warning. "No, probably not. Maybe. I don't know. Maybe The Agent just wants us to know that some sort of danger is connected to this clue." Tasha pulled up a satellite map of Tenebray on her computer so we could study the town and look for the cinderblock walls.

The problem was that there seemed to be a lot of buildings that included cinderblock. The school, the church, the grocery store, the car repair shop, they all had cinderblocks somewhere in their architecture. They also had windows and doors. I magnified the images and searched the map for something we had missed. I slowly moved the map toward northern Tenebray. A square flat roof came into view.

"The Fortress!" yelled Tasha.

"Of course," I answered. We didn't even take time to turn off the computer. We just grabbed our packs and left.

The Fortress was what most kids in Tenebray called the water pump house. The water pump house was a windowless, cinderblock building that was said to house some sort of pumps for the water system. I was never quite sure what that meant, but when I was little the windowless building did in fact look like some kind of impenetrable fortress.

"Cinderblock walls, painted white, no doors or windows in sight," I said once we stood in front of The Fortress. "Now what?" I asked.

"Now we look," said Tasha.

We circled the building several times looking for the symbol of the three swords but found nothing. This no longer discouraged us since the symbol was never easy to find. We just had to keep looking.

"Where's the door?" asked Tasha after our third time around. "I always assumed the door was in the back, but there isn't a door at all. Why would you build a building with no way in?"

"Why would you build a cabin with a door that leads to nowhere?" I asked.

Tasha just shrugged and led us around The Fortress for the fourth time. This time we narrowed our search to the lower part of the building where weeds had grown along its edges. We carefully pulled back every weed to inspect the wall behind it. On the back of the building, the side that faced away from the road, Tasha moved the weeds aside and exposed what looked like a metal foot pedal attached to the building. On top of the pedal was an engraving of the three swords.

We knelt down to inspect it. Tasha gently ran her fingers over the symbol. "Should we push it?" she asked.

"Absolutely," I answered. We stood, and I gently applied pressure to the pedal with my foot. At first nothing happened. But then, once the pedal was fully pressed to the ground, a rectangle of cinderblocks, the size of a door, pushed out from the rest of the wall. The door opened just a crack. Tasha put the tips of her fingers in the opening and pulled. The rectangle of cinderblocks opened on hinges like a doorway. We took a step closer to see what was inside.

There was a staircase going down.

Ten

THE REVENGE OF JEREMIAH PLUM

Tasha took the first step into The Fortress. It was unlike her to be so bold and to move without thinking things through first.

I took out my flashlight. The dusty air floated in the beam of light. The cinderblock walls looked damp and gray. Tasha was standing on a small landing, big enough for two people. The floor was cement. In front of us the stairway descended into darkness.

"Come on," Tasha whispered.

"Are you sure it's safe?" I whispered back.

"We need to do this," she said.

I thought again of my pledge to find justice for Eliza and Basil. Even though they escaped, they had still been treated like criminals—they still spent their lives in fear of being recaptured. I wanted justice for the men who had treated a mother and her child like property.

I stepped over the threshold of The Fortress and followed Tasha down the stairs. I don't know why Tasha felt the strong need to go down those stairs, but I went down for Eliza and Basil.

The stairs descended in a tight spiral. After what seemed to be about four spirals down, we reached another small landing.

"There's something on the wall," said Tasha. I illuminated it with my flashlight. There, hanging on the cinderblock, was a large display case. Inside the case was an old wooden door. The nameplate on the door read, Walker.

"Isn't that the name of the place where Eliza and Basil were held? Didn't they escape from Walker's barn?" I asked.

Tasha nodded. She stood in front of the Walker door for a few seconds and then, without a word, she continued her downward climb into darkness. We went down another set of spirals and another and another until I had no sense of how far we had descended into the earth.

Tasha reached out to me and whispered, "Light."

From where we were standing we could see over the railing to the room below. The room was circular and had a dirt floor. The walls looked to be the same damp cinderblock as the rest of The Fortress. One doorway led into another room. The door to this room was open, and light from the room spilled out into the circular space.

We stepped lightly down the last spiral and onto the packed dirt floor.

"A voice," Tasha whispered.

There were many voices actually — a gathering of people in the illuminated room.

"What do we do?" I whispered.

Tasha looked around and then pulled me back in the direction of the stairs. I assumed she was doing the sensible thing and leading us out of the strange Fortress, but, instead, she crouched on the floor behind the last spiral of stairs. I knelt down beside her. The spirals didn't hide us completely, but I hoped they provided us enough cover in the dim light.

"Let's leave," I said.

"No," said Tasha. "Let's just listen for a minute."

I didn't want to listen. I wanted to leave.

"The family tree is almost complete," a man's voice reported from inside the room. "A few more generations and we will know."

"Ladies and gentleman," another male voice added, "for nearly one hundred and sixty years our order has survived."

Men and women's voices tangled into cheers.

"And," the man continued over the clamor, "for one

hundred and sixty years we have upheld our core principles. Our generation alone has expelled forty from Tenebray."

"Forty what?" I whispered to Tasha.

"I have no idea," she whispered back.

The man continued, "Now, we are merely days away from justice. We are merely days away from righting the sad betrayal of our founder, Jeremiah Plum."

More cheers.

"Jeremiah Plum," I whispered. "Did we just discover the…."

"Shhhh," responded Tasha

"There will be no activity until then," the man's voice commanded. "Not one of us will risk endangering our greatest mission."

There were more cheers and then the voices split into many murmuring conversations.

"It is," said Tasha, answering my earlier question. "I think we just discovered *The Secret Order*."

The slave hunters were still on the prowl.

Eleven

HUNTED

"We need to get out of here before the meeting ends," I whispered.

"We need to see their faces first," Tasha whispered back.

"Are you crazy?" I asked. But she was already up and walking toward the meeting room. What had happened to my friend? She was reckless. I'd never seen her like this before.

I followed her, and we stood at a distance from the doorway. There were about thirty people in the room. They were all seated on folding chairs that had been arranged into three semi-circles. All three semi-circles faced a small stage and a podium. On the floor in front of each semicircle of people was a different symbol. One group had gathered around a triangle, one had gathered around a star, and one had gathered around a square. A triangle, a star, and a square—these were the same shapes that had fallen out of The Agent's first letter to us. It was impossible to identify anyone in the group; the lights were dim and their backs were toward us.

That's when I made the mistake. The floating dust from the floor had been getting to me since we'd descended the spiral staircase. I had been quietly wiping my drippy nose on my sleeve, but standing there, peering into a meeting of *The Secret Order,* I simply forgot. I sniffed my nose.

A woman in the back row turned.

Tasha grabbed my arm. I didn't need to be told what to do. We went back to the stairs, not to hide, but to escape. We ran up the twisting stairs. The dark upward spirals made me sick to my stomach, but we couldn't stop. We had already seen too much, heard too much, risked too much.

I wondered whom *The Secret Order* had expelled. Had they expelled people like Tasha and me, people who had discovered too much? And what did it mean to be expelled from Tenebray?

I could hear footsteps behind us. We climbed faster, but the spiral stairs felt endless, as if we were trapped in a nightmare of infinite steps. It felt like we'd never escape—like we'd never find the top of the windowless Fortress.

We passed the first landing with Walker's door. We

continued the dizzying spiraling up and up and up. And then, like waking from a nightmare, we reached the top landing. The cinderblock door was still ajar, daylight cut through the slit. The dust floated in the light. Tasha pushed the door open and stepped into freedom, but I tripped over the threshold. My shin dragged over the cinderblock. The cement tore into my jeans and then into my skin. The pain was one of those slow rolls, where it doesn't hurt at first but then it rolls in like a crescendo. Silent tears dripped off my face. Even though it was ridiculous, I imagined my dripping tears creating giant pools—a trail for *The Secret Order* to follow, to find us, to hunt us. I thought of the dream I had sometimes where I am trying to scream, but no sound comes out.

Tasha bent down beside me, took my arm, and placed it over her shoulder. She helped me to my feet, and together we hobbled for cover in the forest.

What were they going to do? I wondered. Did they have dogs? Were they going to track us down like they did the runaway slaves? We dropped to the ground behind a fallen tree.

"The door was open," we heard a woman's voice say. "Who was the last one in?"

"Luxen," answered a man.

Ms. Luxen was the librarian who had not let us check out the book on the Civil War. Ms. Luxen was part of *The Secret Order*. The locations with the symbols must have indicated membership in *The Secret Order*.

"Stay here on guard," the woman said. "Report anything unusual."

We peeked over the tree to see what was happening. We saw the woman go back inside. The man leaned against the building with his arms crossed and stared into the forest. We lay down on the forest floor. One thing was clear: we weren't going anywhere for a while.

Twelve

A ONCE HAUNTED LAND

We didn't dare speak. I wondered if this was what it had been like for Eliza and Basil—if they had to hide silently in the forest. But my mind only stayed with Eliza and Basil for a moment before my own fears swelled. The fears that poured in had nothing to do with hiding from *The Secret Order*. Instead I thought about my mom. I had heard her throwing up the night before. I had gotten out of bed to check on her.

"Oh Chloe," she whispered. "I'm so sorry I woke you."

"You okay, Mom?" I said as I handed her a glass of water to wash out her mouth.

"Come lie with me," she said. We went to the couch, and I put my head on her shoulder while she wrapped her arms around me. This had been my favorite place when I was little.

"It's the medicine," she explained in a raspy voice once we had settled. "It makes me sick, but I think that might be a good thing. Maybe that means it's working."

I didn't say anything. Instead I just nestled in closer. Her arms tightened around me.

"Sometimes things have to get bad before they are okay again," she said. "Sometimes there is no other way. The only way to make things okay again is to just go through the bad."

I don't think I really understood what she had meant at the time. But now my mind drifted back to Eliza and Basil, and what my mom had said the night before started to make more sense. The thought of all the miles that stood between them and freedom probably made them sick—all those miles filled with slave hunters and hunger and coldness and uncertainty. Yet they kept going. They did it. I wondered if freedom could be enough to compel any one of us to fight through the bad to get to the good.

It was thirty minutes before we heard the rest of the group emerge. There was very little talking among the departing members. They just went their separate ways back to their hidden lives, back to secretly expelling—whatever that meant—the residents of Tenebray.

Just to be safe we waited another twenty minutes after The Fortress door shut and all of the voices and footsteps disappeared. Then we crept along the edge of the forest to our escape. Every step made my skinned shin pulse with pain.

"*The Secret Order* is still operating," I said to Tasha once I was sure we had put a safe distance between us and The Fortress. "What does that mean? What are they doing? What is expelling?"

"I don't know," answered Tasha.

"Did you see the symbols on the floor?" I asked.

"The same symbols from The Agent's first letter," said Tasha. "Maybe the symbols represent how important they are in the group."

"Remember that star on Jeremiah Plum's door handle?" I asked. "The symbols have to mean something."

Tasha called Filip to see if he had translated anything important. While they talked I thought about how the members of *The Secret Order* had cheered at their plan to bring justice for Jeremiah Plum. How could they call that man their founder? Everything he represented was heinous. He made his money by selling people, people who were vulnerable, a mother and her daughter. And while *The Secret Order* was certainly frightening, I couldn't help but think it also seemed so cowardly—adults hiding in a basement, cheering over their secret cruelty. They were bullies—cowardly, adult bullies.

We walked out of the forested area of Tenebray just as dusk was falling. I felt a sense of relief to be out of the shadows and tangles of the forest and onto the flat open space that stretched out from the forest like an apron. I had been lost in that tangled mess once before. I had slept alone in its darkness. I was happy to be out of its grip.

"Filip will meet us after school tomorrow," Tasha said after she hung up. "You okay?"

"Not really," I answered. "You?"

"Not exactly," Tasha replied. "I'm scared."

I walked home with Tasha and had dinner with her family. After dinner we did our homework together before her mom drove me home. I thanked Mrs. Winthrop for the ride and went inside. The main level was quiet, so I went to the bathroom to clean my wound. The cut wasn't deep, just a long strip of shaved skin. I made myself tolerate the bubbly sting of peroxide and then went upstairs to put on my pajamas. Once changed, I found my parents in their room, my mom asleep in the bed and my dad reading in a chair. My dad held his arms out to me and I went to him for a hug. I let him hold me longer than usual.

"Is she okay?" I whispered.

"I'm fine," my mom answered. "Just tired, sweetie."

I left my dad and crawled into bed next to my mom. She kissed my head and held my hand.

"Where's Jake?" I asked.

"Under here," said a muffled voice from under the bed. "I built a world under the bed. Come see."

I got up and knelt beside the bed to look underneath. I was too big to fit under the bed, but Jake was still small enough to slide under with ease. I found him lying on his belly with a world of cars, dinosaurs, action figures, and airplanes all carefully placed in his under-the-bed world. "I've been under here for three hours and twenty-six minutes," he said, "I timed it." My brother loved time. He was the only six-year-old I knew who always wore a watch. He timed everything: how long it took to brush his teeth, how long it took to walk down the stairs, how long it took my dad to mow the lawn. He kept all those little time statistics in his head. You could ask him at any point how long it took to do something and he could give you the slowest and fastest times.

"I love it," I told him.

"Mom said I could sleep here," he told me. "Wanna sleep with me?"

I wanted to sleep under the bed with my little brother more than anything. The fact that he was under there at all felt a little extraordinary. Jake had always been scared of under the bed. I don't know how many times I checked under beds to assure him nothing scary was there. And, yet, here he was playing in the very spot he used to fear. He had conquered under the bed and changed it to a warm, safe cocoon.

"I don't think I'll fit, buddy," I told him. "I really wish I did though. You made an amazing world down here."

"Maybe you can sleep on the floor next to the bed," Jake suggested. "Mom!" he yelled before I had a chance to respond. "Can Chloe sleep in here, too?"

"Of course," said my mom. "We'll have a family

sleepover." I noticed her voice was weak and crackly, and I could tell that Jake noticed it, too. He laid his head on his hands and stared at a one-legged army man. I reached my arm under the bed and put my hand on his arm. He slid his hand into mine. All I could think of was how Tasha had looked at me when she had said, "I'm scared," because that was exactly how my brother looked—scared. But I knew he wasn't afraid of the make-believe things under the bed.

"Get your pillow," he finally said. "And a blanket. I'll time you, okay?"

I squeezed his hand and went to my room to get my things. Before lying down next to Jake, I sat on my mom's bed to give her a kiss goodnight.

"Thank you," she whispered. "You are a great sister."

"He's a great kid," I said. I meant it.

"Two minutes and thirty seconds if you count the time you spent saying goodnight to Mom," Jake said when I lay down on my spot on the floor beside him.

"Did you say goodnight to Mom?" I asked.

"Yeah," he answered. "I came out when you were getting your stuff. I gave her one of the super hugs."

"Those are my favorite," I said.

"I know," Jake replied. "But I'm saving them for Mom right now.

"That's a good idea," I said.

My dad shut off the light. "You okay, Jake?" he asked. "Are you sure you want to stay under there?"

"Yeah," Jake said with a yawn. "Chloe's here."

"I love you Munchy Bear," I whispered to my little brother.

"I love you too, Go-Go-Chlo," he answered sleepily. I turned and felt the sting of my skinned shin on the blanket. Minutes later I heard Jake's soft, even breaths—like a secret message of hope coming out of a once-haunted land.

Thirteen

WALKER DOOR DAY

The next morning I woke to find Jake's hand reaching out from under the bed and holding my arm. His sweet face was turned toward me. He was asleep and drooling. I quietly giggled and felt a swell of love in my chest. I gently moved out of his grasp to check on my mom. She was asleep as well, but in the dull morning light her skin looked gray.

I think love and fear can feel a lot alike. They both get stuck in your chest, but love makes it easier to breathe and fear feels like the pain of when you swallow a big bite and it gets stuck halfway down.

I left my parent's room, dressed for school, and went into the kitchen where my dad was making breakfast.

"Don't forget I'm having a sleepover at Tasha's tonight," I reminded him.

"Don't forget to call me after school so I know you are there safely," he answered. He brought two plates of his famous cheesy eggs to the table. "Thanks for sleeping with Jake last night," he said after we had started eating. "He had a rough day yesterday."

"Worried about Mom?" I asked.

"Yes."

"Are you worried?" I asked him.

"She'll be fine," he said, although it didn't sound like he believed it. He picked up his fork and then set it down again without taking a bite. He looked so tired. Why hadn't I noticed that before? "Your mom is strong, but it's scary. The thought of losing her is…." He shook his head and didn't finish.

"What are we going to do?" I asked.

"We are going to love her," he said without pause. "Bring her water when she needs it, let her sleep when she is tired, and hold her hand." My dad was on the verge of tears himself. "We are going to love her."

"I love you, Dad," I whispered.

"Oh baby, I love you too," he said.

***

School had been hard since my mom got sick. The days were long and gray and fuzzy and no matter how hard I tried to concentrate, my thoughts of her were always there like a low electric hum inside of me. This day had been extra hard. I still had the fear stuck in my chest.

"You look tired," Tasha said when we met after school. "Did you sleep okay last night?" As we walked to our office I told her about Jake and the sleepover. I didn't mention how Jake used to be terrified of looking under the bed or how my dad had almost cried this morning. But I knew she heard the thing I couldn't quite get myself to say, the thing that was hiding between the letters in all my words, *I'm scared. I'm scared. I'm scared.* I guess after a while good friends can read each other like a secret code.

Filip was waiting for us when we arrived at the office. "My full translation," he said, handing me a packet of typed pages. "Most of it is records of captured runaways and money amounts. But I highlighted everything that had to do with Eliza and Basil."

Tasha and I took the packet to our desk and sat side by side. We paged through the translation until we reached the first highlighted entry.

October 30, 1853

Slave woman, Eliza, and child still at large. Hounds unable to find trail.

November 1, 1853

Search for slave woman, Eliza, and slave child extended to south forest. Still at large.

November 3, 1853

The arrest of Elijah Walker.

"Walker. That's the name from the door," I said to Tasha. "What does Elijah Walker have to do with Eliza and Basil?" I asked Filip.

"Keep reading," he answered.

November 4, 1853

Secret compartment found in floor of Elijah Walker homestead. Mr. Walker formally charged for aiding runaway slaves, Eliza and Basil.

November 9, 1853

Trial of Elijah Walker. Defendant pleads guilty to violating The Fugitive Slave Act. Officer Jeremiah Plum testifies against Mr. Walker.

"Officer Jeremiah Plum?" asked Tasha. "He was a police officer?"

"Yep," said Filip. "I did some research on that. His biography is actually really easy to find since he's listed as the founding father of Tenebray. He was a federal officer. That meant he made bonus money for every slave he caught and returned. My guess is that there was good reason the settlement didn't bother with living near farmland. Jeremiah funded the whole town with his slave hunting. The next settlement was only one mile west. With the kind of money Jeremiah was making, they could simply buy their food from the other settlement instead of growing it themselves."

"No farm work meant more time to hunt slaves," added Tasha.

"It also meant Jeremiah Plum had more control," said Filip. No one had their own food and he controlled all the money. People knew they'd starve without him."

"So people were scared to go against him," I said.

We looked back to the next section of highlighted text.

November 10, 1853

Sentencing of Elijah Walker. By violating The Fugitive Slave Act, Elijah Walker is rightly sentenced to six months in prison and a fine in the amount of $1,000. Prison sentence to commence immediately. Wife and infant daughter of Elijah Walker shall be expelled from the settlement of Tenebray.

"He had a daughter?" I asked. "Elijah Walker had a daughter?"

"Yes," answered Filip.

"Is that why he helped Eliza and Basil? Did he do it because he had a daughter, and he knew how cruel it was to separate Eliza from her own daughter?"

"I don't know," answered Filip. "It doesn't say why he did what he did."

"He went to prison for helping them," I said.

"Yes," answered Filip.

"So he was separated from his own daughter so Eliza could be with hers?"

"It seems that way," said Filip.

"Do you know if Elijah ever made it back to his family?" asked Tasha.

Filip shook his head. "I don't know. There isn't anything else about Elijah's family. But his prison sentence was only six months, so I think we can hope that he found his family when he got out."

"There's that word in here," said Tasha, pointing to the text. "*Expelled*. Just like they used at the secret meeting. I think that means they were kicked out of the town."

"*The Secret Order* said they were still expelling people," I said.

"After what we found out, they'd probably like to expel us," said Tasha.

I wondered exactly how *The Secret Order* went about expelling people. The thought made me feel ice cold.

November 14, 1853

In a ceremonial fashion, the members of Tenebray settlement removed Elijah Walker's door from his homestead and presented it to Jeremiah Plum as their pledge that no slaves would ever again pass through their hands or escape their chains.

"They gave Jeremiah a door as a present?" I asked.
"Keep reading," urged Filip.

November 14, 1854

The settlers of Tenebray gathered today at the home of Jeremiah Plum to stand before Elijah Walker's door and renew their pledge that no slaves shall ever again pass through their hands or escape their chains.

"It's the door to nowhere," Tasha said. "The hinges in Jeremiah's cabin. I bet that's where the door hung for the pledge."

"The same door that now hangs in The Fortress," I added.

November 14, 1855
Walker Door Ceremony

We paged through Filip's translation until we found the next highlight.

November 14, 1856
Walker Door Ceremony

Year after year the entry for November 14 was the same. Every year on November 14, the settlers gathered at Jeremiah Plum's house to renew their pledge to capture and return slaves.

In my mind this whole door thing was as crazy and cowardly as the modern day *Secret Order*. The idea of a group of adults meeting to make a pledge to a mean man and an old door was insane. What a waste. What people could be convinced to pledge their lives to was pretty sad.

"Chloe," Tasha's voice interrupted my thoughts.

"What?" I asked.

"Did you hear me?" she asked. She and Filip were staring at me, looking scared and worried.

"No," I admitted. "Sorry I was daydreaming. What did you say?"

She slid her phone across the desk and pointed at the date.

November 14.

It was Walker Door Day.

Fourteen

IT ISN'T FUNNY

"What do we do?" I asked.

"How about the Historical Society?" suggested Tasha. "What if we ask to check the newspaper records around November 14? Maybe we can figure out if any crimes are committed. I mean, maybe Walker Door Day means they just stand in front of the door."

I should have been comforted at the thought of November 14 being nothing but a ceremonial day, but I wasn't. The thought of that ceremony seemed as horrifying as anything. The thought of people standing in front of that door to nowhere pledging their lives to Jeremiah Plum's mission terrified me.

"It's 4:30," said Filip. "The Historical Society closes at five."

"Then we need to run," said Tasha. "Filip, can you stay here and do Internet searches around the November 14 date?"

"Yep," replied Filip.

"We'll meet back here as soon as Chloe and I finish up."

We grabbed our backpacks and started running.

***

Mr. Spero, an elderly man who often volunteered at the Historical Society, greeted us. "How may I help you young ladies?" he asked.

We stepped into the old house that served as the Historical Society. It smelled musty. "We were wondering if we could look at old newspapers," I asked. "We want to know about things that happened every year around November 14."

Mr. Spero smiled, but something in his smile was off. It was more like a grimace—a smile mixed with amusement and disgust. "Ah," he said with feigned intrigue. "You are researching *The Secret Order*."

The spiders came back. The feeling was so strong I actually looked over my body to make sure it was my imagination. There were no real spiders, but my skin crawled with the memory of them covering me. "You know about *The Secret Order*?" I whispered.

He laughed, but, like his smile, it was off. His laugh was hollow. "Every few years someone comes to research

The Secret Order," he said. You two are hardly the first. And I have to tell you, everyone who comes ends up leaving disappointed when they discover *The Secret Order* is not nearly as sinister as they had hoped."

"Can you tell us about it?" Tasha asked.

"Of course, my dear," he said. "But let's sit; it's the end of the day, and I'm quite tired. You young ones don't understand that yet. You don't understand how tiring it is to be older."

I thought about my dad and how tired he had looked this morning. I thought that maybe grown-up tired wasn't so much about sleepiness, but more about the things you collected in your mind over the years and had to carry. I understood that kind of tired. I carried my mom in my mind a lot.

Mr. Spero led us to a sitting room in the old house. We sat on worn leather armchairs in front of an empty fireplace. The chairs smelled stale. "You have heard of Jeremiah Plum?" Mr. Spero asked once we were seated.

"The founder of Tenebray," Tasha answered.

Mr. Spero smiled and nodded. "Yes. Exactly. Legend has it that Mr. Plum had a tremendous sense of humor. It was one of the reasons he was such a popular leader—everybody loved him. So one day his wife decided to play a joke on him. For years he had complained that their home only had a front door. He didn't like the fact that he had to go out the front door and walk around back when he needed to use the outhouse. He used to tell everybody that when he became a rich man the first thing he was going to do was add a back door to his cabin—an outhouse door.

"So one day, while he was out working in the fields, his wife asked their neighbor, Elijah Walker, to help play a joke on her husband. Elijah agreed. So Mrs. Plum and Mr. Walker hung a door on the inside of the Plum cabin. Now mind you, this wasn't an actual door. It was just a door hung on the wall."

As Mr. Spero talked I noticed that the wooden front of the armchairs were decorated with intricately carved pattern. The pattern was made completely out of triangles.

"That night," Mr. Spero continued, "Jeremiah came home to find the entire settlement of Tenebray crowded in his cabin. His wife ceremoniously presented him with his outhouse door—she said it was a gift from the town. Well, Jeremiah thought it was the greatest thing he'd ever seen. He declared right then and there that he indeed needed to use the outhouse. He walked right to the door, opened it, and nearly walked smack dab into the wall!

"Mr. Plum found the whole thing so funny that he declared November 14, which was of course the date of the practical joke, to be Walker Door Day. It was a bit like April Fools' Day. Every year the funny Mr. Plum had a silly ceremony to salute humor. But Mr. Plum was not to be outdone when it came to a practical joke. So he created a *Secret Order*. His *Secret Order* would meet and plan Walker Door Day jokes. Some say the jokers still meet. Some say there is still a *Secret Order* carrying out funny jokes."

I thought about the meeting at The Fortress. It didn't seem very funny at all.

"Why did they live in northern Tenebray?" asked Tasha. "You said Jeremiah was out in the fields, but the ground there is bad for farming. Why didn't they settle on good land?"

Mr. Spero rolled his eyes. "Such a common misconception," he said. "The northern land was excellent farming at the time. The settlers eventually moved to southern Tenebray because the northern land had become over-farmed."

"But there are the rocks," I said. "That's why it isn't farmable; you can't plow rocks."

"You girls do love to create a mystery, don't you? I'm afraid there is no mystery to be had here. Learn your history before you jump to conclusions." His tone had changed. He was irritated now. "For instance, most of the United States was a dust bowl in the 1930's. It's perfectly farmable now. That land changed. Tenebray's land changed. Land all over the earth changes. Land changes."

"Like I said," he continued. "I'm very tired, and I'm done here for the day. I need to close up and get my tired bones back to the lovely Mrs. Spero. You two need to run along now."

Mr. Spero stood and motioned for us to do the same. "Good day," he said as he ushered us out. He closed the door in our faces and flipped the sign to CLOSED. We heard the deadbolt click.

I didn't know what to think. Mr. Spero had been very believable, and he explained everything. Yet something wasn't right. Too many things, like his smile and his laugh, were just off.

Tasha sat on the front steps of the Historical Society porch. I sat next to her. "It would be a good thing if Mr. Spero was right about this," she said. "It would be good if this was all about jokes. Maybe the joke is on us. Maybe all the letters from The Agent are just part of some practical joke."

"It's not very funny," I said. "What kind of person jokes about slavery and tearing apart a mother and her daughter?"

"I know," said Tasha. "I don't think it's funny either."

"I want to believe Mr. Spero," I said. "It would make everything easier, but it just seems off."

We sat in silence for a few moments, processing the new information. The wind had picked up and turned bitter. Winter wasn't far off. The Historical Society's sign dangled from its post and the iron hooks screeched as metal rubbed against metal. I watched the sign swaying and screeching, and then I saw it.

"Tasha," I whispered. "Look at the sign."

There, within the O of the word *society*, was a faint carving—the three-sword symbol. I turned around and saw Mr. Spero at the window watching us.

Fifteen

THE FIRES

I turned so my back was facing the window. "Mr. Spero is at the window," I whispered to Tasha. "He is watching us."

"Wave," she answered.

"What?" I asked.

"Trust me," she said. "Just smile and act friendly."

I turned and waved to Mr. Spero. I tried to smile, but I was sure it was now my smile that grimaced.

"Mr. Spero!" Tasha called out. "Mr. Spero!"

Mr. Spero unlocked the window and slid it open. "Yes?" His voice was flat and curt.

"I just wanted to thank you for the help," Tasha said.

One corner of Mr. Spero's lip turned up, as if he could only get half of his face to respond—the way a dog growls a warning out of the side of his mouth. "Indeed," said Mr. Spero without humor. "You girls get home now."

"Okay," said Tasha. "Thanks again for all the information. I feel a lot better about it."

Mr. Spero nodded. He closed the window with a slam, turned the lock, and then disappeared into the house.

"He's involved," Tasha whispered to me once our backs were turned. "And he knows we are snooping around."

***

"There have been November 14 fires for the last four years," said Filip when we returned to the office. "Last year there was that brush fire near Parker's Mill. The year before that the Mason's chicken coop burned down. Three years ago on November 14, there was a fire at Sterling's Coffee Shop, and four years ago there was a fire at Bramer's barn."

"Why hasn't anybody noticed this?" I asked.

"All of the fires were ruled to be accidental," answered Filip. So people probably never connected them."

"It's not a coincidence," said Tasha. "I don't believe that for a second. We need to think. What do all of these fires have in common? Are they near each other?"

"No," answered Filip. They are scattered all around Tenebray."

"Can you pull up the news reports?" asked Tasha. "We

need to look for all possible connections. Like, do they all go to the same church, or did the same officer investigate all of the cases? Do their house numbers make some sort of pattern? We need to consider everything if we are going to find a connection."

Filip printed out the news reports. Tasha and I read through them while he searched for more details about each fire. I started with the Bramer fire. The Bramers had owned a thriving horse ranch where they bred and trained horses. Four years earlier one of the horse barns had burned during the night of November 14. Mr. Bramer had only been able to rescue two horses from the barn before the roof caved in. Four horses had been killed in the fire. The Bramers had not rebuilt. Instead they had moved to a new ranch in Calgary.

That was the connection.

"They are all gone," I said.

Filip and Tasha looked up from their work.

"The victims of the November 14 fires are all gone," I explained. "They have all left Tenebray. Joseph Parker sold the mill last spring. Ryan Mason was in our class. His family moved to North Carolina. Edith Sterling left town after her coffee shop burned, and the Bramers moved to Calgary."

"They were expelled," said Tasha. "They expelled Elijah Walker and his family because they went against *The Secret Order*. Maybe that's what they are doing now—expelling people from Tenebray who go against them."

"Then we should be worried," I said.

"Chloe is right," said Tasha. "Nothing stays in the

office tonight. We take home our computers, our files, *The Secret Order* book, and Filip's translation. We have to consider that the office might be a target."

The swish of the paper sliding across the floor was almost inaudible. But it made just enough of a whisper for me to turn my head and see an envelope lying on the floor. I ran to the door and opened it, but, like all the other times, The Agent was nowhere to be seen.

I closed the door and picked up the envelope with its familiar OPEN NOW markings. Inside was a photocopy of what looked like a family tree. The writing was in the same strange symbols as the book. However, under the coded text was a bold warning written in English. I handed it to Filip.

"I left the cipher at home," he said. "I can take it home and call you as soon as I know."

"Just be careful," said Tasha. She pointed to the warning written on the paper. It was scrawled heavily in ink.

BEWARE. SLAVE HUNTERS LURK NEARBY.

Sixteen

ALMOST MIDNIGHT

After Filip left, Tasha and I gathered all of our important files and brought them to the house. I called home to check in with my dad. I could hear Jake playing in the background and his voice gave me a surge of homesickness. Tasha and I had dinner with her parents and then went to work re-reading Filip's translation of *The Secret Order* book. I don't know what we expected to find. We had read those words over and over again and each time it was the same. The book was full of horrible stories from the past, yet it offered no leads of what was to happen next.

I thought about how my dad had spent hours researching cancer on the Internet when my mom first got sick. He even researched while we ate dinner. I don't know what he expected to find, but whatever it was, I don't think he ever found it. One evening during dinner he just closed his laptop and put his head in his hands. He sat like that for several minutes. Jake and I stopped eating. I'm not sure why, but it just felt like we needed to be still for him. After a few minutes he sat up, put his laptop away, and we finished dinner together. I never saw him researching cancer again.

"I think we need to take a break," I said. "I don't think we are going to find what we need."

We left *The Secret Order* book in Tasha's room and went downstairs to the kitchen. It was late, nearly eleven-thirty. Tasha's parents were in the family room watching a movie. I sat at the counter while Tasha made popcorn.

"What if Mr. Spero was right?" I asked when Tasha sat down. He had put enough doubt in my mind to make me question what was real. "Could this all be a joke?"

"He was really convincing," answered Tasha. "But we've got to stick with the evidence and not just our feelings. Think about it. Could the soil in northern Tenebray really just turn to rock? Grass doesn't even grow in some places; it's pure rock."

"True," I agreed.

"And," she continued, "if this was a joke then it would be a really expensive joke. Did someone build The Fortress as a joke? Did they make the secret cinderblock door as a joke? Did they make Jeremiah Plum's fireplace as a joke? Not likely."

"True."

"But more than anything, it's like you said before. It isn't funny. We are talking about really awful things—slavery, selling people for money—if this is a joke it is still wrong. Nothing about it is funny."

"Still," I said, "it's easier to just believe Mr. Spero than to believe that something so horrible exists in Tenebray."

"Maybe that's why *The Secret Order* lasted so long," said Tasha. "For that exact reason. It's just easier to ignore it than to fight it."

"Do you want more popcorn?" I asked. "I can make some."

"Definitely," answered Tasha.

I walked around the counter, put popcorn in the microwave, and then stood at the window looking into the cold, dark night. The wind howled like it was wounded. In the small glint of moonlight, I saw something move and then disappear behind Tasha's barn.

I thought of the night I had spent alone in Tenebray Forest, how everything and nothing looked frightening—I thought about how the shadows and the trees and the wind had mixed up what was real and what was my imagination. I knew that things changed in the darkness. Had I seen a person near the barn? Or was it a shadow? I stood, covered in tiny tingles like the legs of the spiders, uncertain of what was real.

"Chloe?" Tasha was beside me holding a bag of

burnt popcorn. "Are you okay?"

I looked at the bag of popcorn. The paper had browned and burned and the kitchen was full of the rancid smell of smoke. "Sorry," I said. "I got distracted."

"It's okay," said Tasha. "We have more popcorn."

I didn't say anything.

"Do you want to just go to sleep?" she asked. "I'm not sure what else we can do. It is almost midnight, almost November 15. Whatever they were planning has probably already happened."

I looked at the clock. 11:53. Seven minutes until November 15. My mind skipped back and forth between feelings and evidence, uncertain of where to land or what to believe.

Tasha stood at the window with me. "Chloe?" she asked. "Chloe? Are you okay?"

"I don't know," I whispered. "Something's not right." Maybe it was just the dark night, maybe it was the howling wind, maybe it was my imagination, or maybe, just maybe there were things to fear out by the barn. I looked at the clock. 11:54. Six minutes until November 15. "Let's just wait until midnight," I said.

"Okay," she said and quietly stood next to me.

11:55.

Five minutes until November 15.

11:56.

Four minutes until November 15.

11:57.

Three minutes until November 15.

11:58.

Tasha gasped and clutched my arm.

There were three men standing by the barn.

Seventeen

EXPELLED

"Dad!" Tasha screamed as she made a dash for the family room. "Dad! Dad!"

Mr. Winthrop met us in the hallway, looking dazed by his daughter's screams. "Tasha?" he asked. "What's wrong? Are you okay?"

"There are people out there," Tasha yelled. "By the barn!"

"What's going on?" Mrs. Winthrop asked, rushing out of the family room.

"We saw three men standing by the barn," answered Tasha.

Mr. Winthrop pushed past us and into the kitchen. We started to follow him, but he stopped us and made us wait in the hallway. He turned off the kitchen lights and looked out toward the barn.

"Are they still there?" asked Tasha.

"Yes," Mr. Winthrop answered.

"Who are they?" I asked.

"I don't know," he answered. "Call the police," Mr. Winthrop said to Tasha's mom. He went to the back door to put on his shoes.

"Where are you going?" Tasha asked her dad.

Mr. Winthrop didn't answer.

"Dad, are you going out there?" Tasha asked. She started walking toward him.

"Tasha," he said firmly. "Stay here."

"But, Dad," she argued.

My phone rang from my back pocket. I looked at the screen. It was Filip. "I can't talk right now," I said into the phone instead of, "Hello."

"Dad," said Tasha, "Don't go out there!" She sounded close to tears.

Filip said something, but I was listening to Mrs. Winthrop talking to the police on her phone.

"What?" I said absentmindedly.

"The family tree is Eliza's!" Filip shouted.

"Filip," I said firmly, "this is a bad time. I have to call you back."

"No!" he said frantically.

"Dad!" Tasha screamed, "Please don't go out there. Please wait for the police!"

Filip was still talking in my ear. "Filip, this has to wait," I told him.

But he kept talking. "Eliza," he said, "she hid in plain sight. She hid in Tenebray Forest. She lived there. She even got married."

"Filip," I said with irritation. "Not now."

But he was adamant, "It can't wait, Chloe."

Mr. Winthrop ignored Tasha's pleas and opened the back door. "Hey!" he yelled into the dark night. "Get out of here!"

"Don't you get it?" asked Filip.

I had missed what he had said. "Get what?" I asked.

"I said Eliza married a man named, Luke Winthrop."

"So?" I said to Filip.

"Winthrop. She married a man with the last name Winthrop."

"So Tasha is...."

"A descendant of Eliza," said Filip. "*The Secret Order* has been looking for revenge for one hundred and sixty years. I think they are going to do something to the Winthrops tonight!"

From where I was standing I could now see at least four figures moving near the barn. "Filip," I said, "there are people here now—out by the barn!"

There was a woosh of wind like a giant exhale. The four men lit large torches and positioned themselves around the barn. At the exact same time they held their torches to the walls and then moved clockwise like a sick game of ring-around-the-rosy.

"They are lighting the barn on fire!" Mrs. Winthrop yelled into her phone.

"Chloe! What is happening?" Filip kept yelling. "What's happening?"

I ignored him. "The family tree!" I screamed to Tasha. "Filip decoded it. Eliza was a Winthrop!"

"What?" asked Tasha.

"A Winthrop!" I screamed. "This is about Eliza and the escape. Your family is the target!"

The fire took hold and slowly licked its way across the barn. The figures of the men were illuminated in an amber glow. There was no hiding now, no secrets, just an open display of cinders and hate. As the fire grew, so did the light. I clearly saw the face of one of the men—his face contorted in a familiar grimace. It was Mr. Spero.

Eighteen

THE FACE OF HATE

Sirens screamed in the distance as the fire grew rapidly and ate the barn in crackling licks. Each of the men shattered a barn window with his torch. Mr. Spero paused to smile at us before throwing his torch through a broken window into the barn. The other three men followed suit before running to hide in the woods behind Tasha's house. I thought again about the cowardly face of hate. For one hundred and sixty years *The Secret Order* had taken advantage of the weakest among them and called it power. But I knew better. I knew I wasn't witnessing power. I was witnessing cowardice.

The police were the first to arrive. Mr. Winthrop met them in the driveway and showed them where the men had run. The officers pursued the men and released tracking dogs into the woods. The hunters had now become the hunted.

The Winthrops and I stood on the back porch, helpless against the flames. I heard the fire truck siren in the distance, but I knew they weren't going to make it in time. The fire crawled and roared through the roof of the barn as if it were alive, as if it were hungry and ravenous—eating its revenge. The night air was thick with the fire's rank odor. The skunky smell of burning hay mixed with the stale smell of old burning wood. I knew the smell was seeping into my hair and my clothes and each inhale burned with noxious smoke.

The fire truck howled down Tasha's street, it's lights twirling and bumping off the houses. The firemen drove onto the lawn as the barn roof cracked and snapped like bones and fell into the fiery center of the barn. The firemen exited the truck like soldiers and soon shot beams of water into the inferno. The fire hissed at them like an angry animal and puffed seething billows of white steam and smoke into the air.

Police dogs barked in the distance.

The Winthrops and I stood huddled and shaking in the cold night. Neighbors began to gather, their voices murmuring into the darkness. Someone wrapped a large blanket around us.

When the firemen finally quenched the fire, all that was left was a collapsed frame and smoldering, black ash.

Nineteen

LIGHT

A firefighter asked to speak to Mr. and Mrs. Winthrop in private. Tasha's parents moved out of our huddle. Tasha and I sank to the ground, and Mrs. Winthrop wrapped the blanket around us before she left.

"You are related to Eliza and Basil," I said. "That's pretty amazing."

"I wouldn't be here if she hadn't escaped with Basil," said Tasha. "I look into those dark woods right now and I know those men are out there somewhere. I'd be terrified to go in there. But think about it, Eliza and her daughter chose to go into the dark woods with slave hunters trying to find them."

I tried to imagine the reality of a runaway slave—running and hiding and being hunted. "I don't know if I would have had the guts to try," I admitted.

Flashlight beams shone out of the woods like headlights. The police officers emerged with four men in handcuffs. Mr. Spero had neither a smile nor a grimace. Instead, he looked small and old. He looked weak. Without a secret building or anyone to bully, Mr. Spero just looked like a coward.

The four men looked away from the crowd that had gathered. They tried to hide their faces, but it was useless. There were angry shouts and shocked murmurs as people began to recognize the four men and the crime they had committed.

Tasha stood and took her phone from her pocket. She walked toward the four handcuffed men—the men who represented all the hate and secrecy we had uncovered. She went to each man, one by one, and held her phone toward their faces. One by one she snapped their pictures. Four bright flashes of light, four images burned into memory, four pictures revealing the faces of Tenebray's most heinous secrets. I understood exactly what she was doing. *The Secret Order* had continued because its members had done cruel things in secret. They had gotten away with expelling people because they kept their faces hidden. When Tasha took their pictures, she ended the hiding and secrecy. *The Secret Order* had finally been brought to light.

Twenty

QUIET

My dad came to take me home. The first thing I did when I got there was take a long, hot shower. I washed my hair three times, but the smell of smoke would not go away.

I put on my pajamas and went into my parent's room. My dad was sitting in his chair, reading. He motioned for me, and I went to him and sat on his lap like a child.

"Is Jake under the bed?" I asked.

My dad nodded. I stood and walked to the bed. I knelt down to look under. Jake was sleeping in his under-the-bed world—the place of fear that he had overcome.

"Chloe?" my mom whispered.

"Right here Mom," I answered. I stood and held her hand.

"Are you okay?" she asked. "Dad told me what happened."

My mom's skin was gray and she had dark circles under her eyes. The chemo treatments had caused her hair to fall out. She hardly looked like my mom, she looked more like a smooth shell of what she had once been. I didn't answer. Instead I climbed into bed with her and we snuggled under the covers—a place that felt untouched by the relentless push of cancer.

"I know you are afraid," my mom whispered. "But I think I'm getting better. I can feel it. It might take a while, but we are going to be okay again." She kissed the top of my head and snuggled me in closer.

In that cocoon of warmth I understood that *The Secret Order* wasn't true power. Powerful things were quieter, like the low hum of electricity through power lines. Real power and strength looked more like Eliza and Basil and felt like my mother's arms.

I closed my eyes and listened to Jake's quiet and restful breaths coming from beneath the dark and conquered bed.

Twenty-One

FREEDOM

The next morning my dad drove me to Tasha's house. He went to talk to Mr. Winthrop, and I found Tasha sitting in our office, staring out the window.

"You okay?" I asked.

"Not really," she answered. "I keep thinking about Eliza. Did she understand when she escaped that she was freeing more than Basil, more than herself. I mean, I'm here because a hundred and sixty years ago, a woman named Eliza did something brave. In a way she freed me, too."

"I think you are a lot like her," I said. "I was so scared when we were in The Fortress. I wanted to leave so badly, but you kept going."

"I was scared, too."

"Yeah, but I don't think being scared has anything to do with it. I'm sure Eliza was scared, but she kept running north. She kept going. So did you."

"Think we'll ever find out who The Agent is?" she asked.

"I hope so," I answered. "Maybe someday he'll let us know with another OPEN NOW. It makes sense now why he was so secretive. He probably was scared of being expelled,"

"Like me," said Tasha. "They tried to expel my family."

I walked up behind her and saw that she had been staring out the window at the burnt, skeleton-like remains of the barn.

"It's hard to believe that people could hate us this much." She nodded toward the barn. "I keep thinking about Mr. Spero. He sat there across from me with all of that hate, just because of who my great-great-great-great grandmother was."

"I'm sorry this happened to you," I said. I sat down in the chair next to her.

"What if someone comes back?" asked Tasha.

There it was again, the lingering fear, the spiders that weren't there, the things under the bed, the reason to stay afraid. "I heard that Detective Clauge was working on the case," I said.

Tasha nodded. "Mr. Spero ended up giving Detective Clauge the names of everyone in *The Secret Order*. He said they have arrested everyone. You know those shapes that we saw on the floor of The Fortress?"

I nodded.

"Mr. Spero said that each member of *The Secret Order* was categorized into one of three shapes. The stars were the leaders of *The Secret Order*. They told everyone what to do. The squares did things like research people they wanted to hurt. They are the ones who figured out my family tree. Mr. Spero was in the triangle group. The triangles are the ones who went out and did the bad things like light our barn on fire."

"I'm glad Detective Clauge is working on it," I said. "I'm sure he'll stop all of them. You have nothing to worry about anymore."

Tasha didn't say anything, and I knew that this was like the day of the spiders. Tasha told me a million times that they were gone, but it didn't matter; I was still afraid. And now it didn't matter how much I reassured Tasha that she was safe; she was just plain afraid.

I didn't know what to say, so I just put my arms around Tasha and hugged my best friend. She has never given up on me, and I was never going to give up on her. As we hugged I thought about how Eliza kept going for Basil. I thought about how my mom keeps fighting and being strong for me. It occurred to me that relentless and unending love is stronger than any *Secret Order,* or cancer, or even the imaginary things we fear under the bed. True power isn't always the biggest or loudest or scariest thing in the room. Sometimes true power simply looks like love that refuses to give up.

Twenty-Two

THE BOX

Three weeks later Tasha and I sat in our office after finishing up a missing dog case. After *The Secret Order*, dealing with a lost dog felt like a vacation. But somehow, it still felt important. There is nothing better than watching the joy that comes when you hand someone her lost pet.

Carpenters were busily hammering and sawing outside our office. The Winthrops had decided to rebuild the barn. Even though the rubble had been taken away, the earth still looked charred—like a scar from that horrible night.

With all the construction noise, we almost didn't hear the soft tapping on our door. I opened it to find a sweet little girl holding a box. I invited her in and offered her a seat.

Tasha asked how we could help her. I assumed she came to report a lost pet. We had a steady stream of kids come through our office and that was always their problem.

So I didn't expect what happened next.

The young girl stood, opened the box, and held it out for us to see.

Tasha and I looked inside. Then we looked at each other in disbelief.

"Now you understand," said the girl. "I need your help."

Hey Everybody,

Tasha and I found out that slavery didn't just end when it became illegal in the United States and Canada. We discovered that there are millions and millions of slaves all over the world, right now—even in North America. Slavery is illegal all over the world, but that hasn't stopped some individuals from doing really bad things by capturing people and making them their slaves.

After learning about Eliza and Basil's history, we knew that it wouldn't be right for us to just look the other way and do nothing about modern day slavery. We found out that there were a lot of things we could do as kids to help, so we decided to start an Abolitionist Movement in our school (an abolitionist is someone who works to end slavery).

We started by hanging a bunch of posters all over school to get everyone's attention. Our first meeting is next week, Wednesday. Feel free to copy our posters and start an Abolitionist Movement in your own school!

Love,
Chloe

P.S. Visit www.gemsgc.org/mrm to download and use our posters in your school!

SLAVERY STILL EXISTS!

There are currently between 12 and 27 million people in slavery around the world.

>>> US Department of State

HELP END SLAVERY!

Join us for our first Abolitionist Meeting Wednesday at 3:30 in the Library!

KIDS IN SLAVERY

DID YOU KNOW THAT THERE ARE AT LEAST 5.5 MILLION KIDS IN SLAVERY RIGHT NOW?
>>> ILO

Some kids are forced to be soldiers and fight in wars. Some kids are forced to work dangerous jobs. Many child slaves are taken from their families. Child slaves are treated terribly.

These are kids just like you.
WE NEED TO HELP FREE THESE KIDS!

Join us for our first Abolitionist Meeting Wednesday at 3:30 in the Library!

HOW YOU CAN HELP!

★ Talk about it! When more people know about modern day slavery, more people can help.

★ Support an organization that works to free slaves. Did you know you can raise money to purchase a slave's freedom?

★ In some countries slaves are used to process sugar, coffee, cocoa, and clothing. Those things end up in North America, and we end up buying things made by slaves! This is the Fair Trade logo. Products with this logo are guaranteed to be 100% slave free.

FIND OUT MORE!
Join us for our first Abolitionist Meeting Wednesday at 3:30 in the Library!

Glossary

Abolitionist — A person who works to end slavery.

African Slave Trade/Transatlantic Slave trade — The kidnapping of people from Africa and the transportation of them to Europe and North America to be sold as slaves.

Fugitive Slave Act of 1850 — An act passed by the United States Congress stating that slaves who escaped to free states could be hunted down and returned to their slave owners. It also punished people who tried to help runaway slaves.

Human Trafficking — The act of selling human beings and forcing them to do things against their will.

Modern Day Slavery — The term used to describe slavery that exists in our world today.

Slavery — A system in which people are bought and sold like property. Slaves are forced to work without pay and are not allowed to leave.

Slave Hunters — People who make money by hunting down and returning runaway slaves to their owners.

Underground Railroad — A secret network of North Americans who helped slaves escape to freedom.

Crack the Code!

USE FILIP'S CIPHER TO CRACK THE CODE

Filip's Cipher

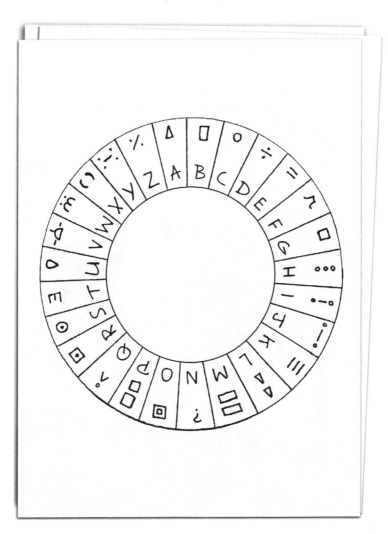

Order Book One!

If you loved *The Secret Order*, you won't want to miss the book that started it all!

When a boy is accused of committing a crime in the shadowy Tenebray Forest, all evidence points to his guilt. He turns to *The Micah Road Detective Agency* for help. Tasha and Chloe take his case only to find they have taken on something bigger and more frightening than what they feel capable of handling.

Visit www.gemsgc.org/mrm to order online.

SHINE brightly Magazine

You don't have to wait for the next book to keep up with the adventures of Tasha and Chloe. Follow their mysteries in **SHINE** *brightly* Magazine. **SHINE** *brightly* is a magazine created for girls ages 9-14. Order your subscription today!

For more information or to order online visit www.gemsgc.org.

Dear Readers,

I was in second grade when I read my first book about slavery in North America. I couldn't believe something so horrible had existed. I went on to read book after book about life as a slave and about the heroes who worked to free them—heroes like Harriet Tubman, Abraham Lincoln, and the nameless people who risked their own freedom by working *The Underground Railroad*.

As a kid I wished I could have lived back then so I could have proven myself as someone courageous and brave enough to be a part of something like *The Underground Railroad*.

But what I've come to realize is that it doesn't matter when we live, there are always opportunities to stand up against things that are wrong. Millions of children are currently enslaved around the world. Millions of young people, just like you, are taken from their parents and bought and sold like property. Imagine what that must be like.

I want to hear your stories about ending slavery. Did you use Tasha and Chloe's posters in your school? Did you raise money? Did you use your voice to tell people about what is going on? Email me with your activism steps and ideas about ending slavery. I'll share your stories and ideas on my website: www.gemsgc.org/mrm.

Together our voices can make a difference.

Hugs,
Sara Lynne Hilton

Email your stories to micahroad@gemsgc.org